Ms. Fely Presents John and the Banana

Fely Heinz

Illustrated by
Christina Cartwright

AuthorHouse™
1663 Liberty Drive
Bloomington, IN 47403
www.authorhouse.com
Phone: 1 (800) 839-8640

Published by AuthorHouse 04/24/2019

ISBN: 978-1-5462-7860-3 (hc)
ISBN: 978-1-5462-7861-0 (sc)
ISBN: 978-1-5462-7862-7 (e)

Library of Congress Control Number: 2019901215

Print information available on the last page.

This book is printed on acid-free paper.

authorHOUSE®

One Monday morning, the sun was shining brightly, the sky was blue, and John was ready to go to school. "John, are you ready for your first day of school?" asked his mom. "Yes, Mommy, and I'm excited to meet my new friends and see Ms. Fely, my teacher!"

On the way to school, John asked his mom, "What will it be like at school?" "Well, school is fun. It's big, and it has a huge playground. The classrooms have cool stuff, and the teachers are awesome." "Really, Mommy?" he asked. "Yes! And you will also have lunch there with your friends." "Now I can't wait to be at school!" John's face was full of excitement, and he asked his mom, "Are we there yet, Mommy?" "I'm just about to pull into the parking lot now," his mom said. "Hurray!" John exclaimed.

When they got inside the school, John was amazed by what he saw. "Wow, this school is big!" "Yes, it is John!" Ms. Fely said. John wondered whose voice that was; he turned around, and there he saw Ms. Fely. "Hi, Ms. Fely." "Hello, John. How are you?" "I'm good." And how are you, Ms. Rita?" "I am doing great, thank you," his mom said. "So, are you ready to see your classroom, John?" "Yes, I am, Ms. Fely!" And John waved goodbye to his mom.

While Ms. Fely and John walked down the hallway toward the classroom, John grabbed Ms. Fely's hand and held it tight. Ms. Fely looked at John and said, "You are going to be okay." John looked at her and smiled.

Ms. Fely opened the door of her classroom, and John was surprised to see the classroom. There were great posters on the wall, that showed the letters of the alphabet, numbers, shapes, and colors. "This is awesome; I love it here!" said John. Ms. Fely smiled when she heard that.

As John looked around the classroom, he saw that he and Ms. Fely were the only ones there. He walked up to Ms. Fely's table and asked her, "Where are all my new friends?" "Are they coming?" John looked sad because even though the classroom had a lot of cool stuff, he was the only kid.

Ms. Fely saw John's sad face and said, "John, don't be sad. Your friends are coming! And besides, it is still early; that's why it's just you who is here right now." "They will start coming in a minute; you'll see." "Really?" he asked. Ms. Fely told John to just wait and see because the classroom would be full of children soon.

A minute later, the door opened wide. A little girl ran toward Ms. Fely and gave her a hug. “Good morning, Madelyne; how are you?” “I am good, Ms. Fely; thank you!” At the door, Madelyne’s mom said, “Goodbye, Madelyne; you have a great day. See you later!” “Bye, Mommy. I love you.”

When John saw Madelyne, he got a smile on his face because finally there was another child in the classroom. Madelyne said, "Hello. What is your name?" "My name is John, and what is your name?" John asked. "I'm Madelyne." While John and Madelyne were talking, more children arrived.

Ms. Fely said, "See John?" "There are more children coming. Do you feel better now?" John had a huge smile on his face and said, "Yes, Ms. Fely, and I can't wait to play with them!"

As morning turned into afternoon. Ms. Fely asked John whether he had a good day. John said that he did have a good day and enjoyed playing with his friends, especially Madelyne, who was nice to him. He also said that he couldn't wait till tomorrow because school was just fun. While John was talking to Ms. Fely, John's mom came. Ms. Fely said, "It is good to know that you had fun today. I'll see you tomorrow. Look; your mom is here." John said, "Goodbye, Ms. Fely," as he walked out the door.

When John got home, he told his mom, "I had so much fun at school today playing with my new friends, and my teacher is really nice." "That's awesome, John," his mom said.

The following morning at school, John played with Madelyne. They built blocks together and had a good time. John said, “This is fun! Let’s play again this afternoon.”

The bell rang, and Ms. Fely said, "It's time to clean up and get ready for the lesson on the carpet."

On the carpet, before Ms. Fely started her lesson, she read a book. "Okay, class, I am going to read you a story called "*The Banana*." The children got excited when they heard that, and Madelyne asked Ms. Fely, "Why is it called "*The Banana*?" "Madelyne, you will know why if you will listen, and I want everybody else to do the same. Understood?" "Yes, ma'am!" the children replied with enthusiasm.

Ms. Fely was about to turn to the first page when John suddenly said, "I love bananas. They are my favorite fruit!" Everyone looked at John and then back at the book. "I love bananas too, John, but I need to read this book now," Ms. Fely said.

Everyone was paying attention as Ms. Fely read the first sentence. *"One Friday morning, Kyle was having breakfast at home with his family. On his plate, he had scrambled eggs, bread, and half of a banana."*

"Kyle put the banana in his mouth and ate very fast, and then he started choking! When his mom saw Kyle choking, she patted his back hard enough for Kyle to start spitting the banana out of his mouth."

"The family got worried, and even Kyle himself got nervous and cried. His mom gave him a hug to make him feel better and said, 'If the banana could talk, it would tell you to take one bite at a time so that you will not choke and not to put a big piece of it in your mouth." "So next time, you need to remember to take one bite at a time, okay, Kyle?" "Yes, Mommy, I will." Kyle replied with a small voice."

As Ms. Fely continued reading the book, everyone listened attentively. But the children were a little surprised by what happened to Kyle as she finished the story. "Did you like the story?" "Yes, I did. Ms. Fely," said Madelyne. And so, did the other children! "So, what was the story all about?" John raised his hand and said, "The story was about Kyle, who choked on a banana." "That's right, John very good!"

Right after carpet time, it was lunch-time. "Okay, children, I would like you to make a line to wash your hands for lunch." All the children lined up to go to the bathroom. As they were lining up, John said to Madelyne, "I am very hungry and want to eat now." "Lunch will be here soon," she said.

After they had washed their hands, the lunch lady brought food. "Your lunch smells good," Ms. Fely said. "What's for lunch, Ms. Fely?" asked one of the children. "You will have chicken nuggets, mac and cheese, and some tropical fruits."

Everyone said, "I love chicken nuggets and mac and cheese!" Madelyne got her plate first, and then John got his. The classroom got quiet as everyone was about to eat.

John picked up a chicken nugget with his fork and put the whole nugget in his mouth while Madelyne was taking one bite at a time with her nuggets.

Suddenly, John started choking. Ms. Fely heard it, and when she looked at the children, she realized it was John. She hurriedly walked toward him and as she was about to pat his back, John coughed the pieces of nugget out of his mouth.

Everyone in the classroom was looking at John with worry on their faces, and a few of the children stood up to watch. Ms. Fely stroked John's back softly as he was calming down and said, "Okay, John, let's go to the sink to clean your face and wash your hands."

As Ms. Fely held John's hand to take him to the bathroom, she seemed calm. She helped John clean his face and gave him a bear hug afterwards. She told him, "You're going to be okay."

Then she took John back to his chair and let him finish his food. Madelyne said to John, "Remember about the story *The Banana*?" "You need to take one bite at a time and not eat too fast so that you will not choke." Ms. Fely said, "That's right, Madelyne!" And John said, "Okay, Ms. Fely, I will take one bite at a time when I eat my food and will eat slowly." "I am glad to hear that, John!" Ms. Fely said.

When the children were done eating, Ms. Fely looked at all the children and said, "What happened to Kyle in the story and to your friend John was not good. It's scary, and I hope that will not happen again to anybody else."

The next day, John and his family were having dinner, and he sat next to his big sister, Victoria. "I heard about what happened to you at school during lunch yesterday. I'm glad you're okay little brother." John just listened to Victoria and nodded, agreeing with his sister.

When Victoria picked up her hot dog, John looked at his sister and said, "Remember: take one bite at a time so that you will not choke like me and Kyle." Victoria said, "Yes, I know, John, because I read that book, "*The Banana*", when I was in second grade."

When John's mom heard what he said, she smiled and told John. "I'm glad you learned something." "Yes, Mommy," John said. And from then on, John always remembered what happened to him and made sure to take one bite at a time.

The End